George and Amy's Great Adventure.

Dedicated to my grandchildren

a constant source of

Joy, happiness, laughter and love.

October 2017.

CHAPTER ONE.

Amy saw it first, a flash of reflected sunlight as the clouds drifted away from the afternoon sun. It was gone just as quick, as another cloud covered the sun. "Did you see it, George?" She asked her brother.

"See what, Amy?"

"A flash of light on the grass."

"I didn't see anything." He replied, just as the cloud cleared the sun.

"There!" Shouted Amy, "Up there"

"Now I see it." Cried George and they both ran towards the flashing light. This time the clouds were kind and stayed away from the sun so they were able to go right up to the source of the mysterious flashing light.

Amy stooped and picked up a gold ring with an enormous diamond set in red claws. Inside the ring they could see engraved letters: LA PATRIA ES PRIMERO. "What does it say?" Asked Amy.

"I don't know." Said, George, "It's French or Spanish, or maybe Latin."

Amy frowned, "Latin?"

"The language the Romans used a thousand years ago and is sometimes used today for mottos."

"How can we find out?" Amy said.

They looked at each other for a few moments and then, as one, both said, "GOOGLE."

They carefully wrapped the ring in a handkerchief, George stuffed it in his pocket and they ran to join their Mum and Dad sitting on the nearby bench.

"Look what we found." They said together, "Can we go home and Google that writing?"

Their Mum and Dad looked at the ring and the inscription and nodded, "Come along then, no time like the present." And they all set off for home.

It didn't take long. Google identified the inscription as the National Motto of Mexico and translated into English it read as, 'The Homeland is First.'

"Can I keep it?" asked Amy. Dad smiled, "First of all, Amy, we need to find out if it's real, and then if anyone has reported it lost or stolen."

George jumped to his feet, "I know how to find out if it's real" and rushed out the room returning a few moments later with Dad's shaving mirror. "Diamonds are supposed to be the hardest thing of all, hard enough to cut glass... can we try?"

Dad nodded and picked up the ring and ran it across the mirror expecting not for one second anything would happen so he was absolutely astounded when it left a deep gash in the mirror.

"My goodness me, it looks as if we have a real diamond here."

"Turn on the television news, see if there is anything about a lost ring." Mum suggested.

Well, of course, all of us know we should always listen to Mum because no sooner had they turned on the television then a story appeared about the visit of the President of Mexico. They all looked at one another and Dad turned up the sound to make sure they missed not a single word of the report.

The news moved on to other matters at home and overseas and Dad was about to turn it off when Mum said, "No. Leave it on just in case there is anything else." Mum was right again because the last item was one that made them all sit up and lean forward.

The Mexican President and his family were staying as guests of the British Prime Minister at his country home, CHEQUERS, a beautiful Elizabethan manor house in Buckinghamshire less than ten miles from where George and Amy lived.

The President and his family had been sitting in the garden having tea with the Prime minister and his wife; it was a glorious day with bright sun and blue sky. They were admiring jewellery the President had brought to England for ceremonial use, a magnificent ring in a velvet lined case was sitting in pride of place on the table, sunlight twinkled off its diamond; suddenly a shadow had flitted across the jewellery and those sitting at the table but it was not a cloud, a magpie had swooped down, clutched the ring in its claws and flew off before anyone could react.

The magpie and ring were gone. A distraught President expected to never see the ring again, a valuable and historically important artefact, presented to Mexico by the King of Spain in 1821 in recognition of its independence from Spain. A full description of the ring followed including the engraved motto.

The telephone operator at 10 Downing Street was very helpful. She listened to everything Amy's Dad said but was unable to provide a telephone number for Chequers, however she would contact the Prime Minister's country residence and leave details of this telephone conversation. He put the 'phone down and turned to George and Amy. "That's all we can do for now so why don't you two scoot upstairs and get ready for..." The ringing of the telephone stopped him mid-sentence.

The telephone call was from Chequers. The personal aid of the Mexican President or more accurately the very excited personal aid of an excited President and if they sent a limousine in the morning would the family be available to travel to Chequers to meet the President and his family and stay for lunch.

George and Amy, as well as Mum and Dad arrived at Chequers in a long stretch limousine complete with a small Mexican flag flying on its radiator grill. They were greeted at the door by a butler and shown through to a, magnificent drawing room where they were presented to the Mexican President and his wife. A smiling and confident Amy walked towards the President and handed him a square of silk. The President carefully unfolded the silk to reveal the ring. He smiled, took Amy's hand, kissed it and said, "Gracias mi pequeño"

"Thank you, my little one" the President's wife translated in a hushed whisper.

They enjoyed a wonderful day at Chequers that included a tour of the house and grounds, a game of croquet, a delicious lunch and a knockabout on the tennis court. They even met the Prime minister who took time to look in on them before he left for Westminster.

As they were preparing to leave, the President said to Mum and Dad. "You have every reason to be very proud of your children; finding my ring and bringing it to you was a sign of great integrity and maturity. My country and I are in your debt; we would like to show our appreciation by having you visit our country as my personal guests. We have much to show you, there is much to see. Please say yes. It is the least we can do."

And that is how and why George and Amy went to Mexico and what was to became their Great Adventure.

* * *

CHAPTER TWO

The big jet touched down in Mexico twelve hours after it had taken off from London airport. Twelve long, boring, bottom-numbing hours surrounded by noisy people, screaming babies, terrible food and long queues for the toilets.

But NOT for George and Amy or Mum and Dad.

They had all turned left when they boarded the aircraft, in other words they were travelling First-Class as guests of the Mexican Government; Big seats that would lay flat if they wanted to sleep. Big TV screens so that they could watch films, play games or follow the route of the aircraft as it crossed the ocean towards Mexico but best of all was the wonderful food and the special care and attention lavished on them by the cabin crew who treated them like Royalty.

First class was not busy in fact there was only three other people travelling that day, a famous American film star who was happy to sit and chat with Mum and Dad but for George and Amy it was the other two who helped while away the hours. They were both Russian, the woman had been a Prima Ballerina with the World famous Bolshoi Ballet; now, long since retired she taught at various schools around the world when she wasn't accompanying her husband, a Grand Master chess player and the current World champion.

Amy was entranced by the dancer who regaled her with stories of life as ballerina and the dedication required to achieve success.

George was amazed when the man removed a chess board from his case and suggested they have a game. There then followed three hours of play and tuition that unquestionably improved George's understanding and knowledge of the game.

Just before the Captain announced they were approaching Mexico City, the flight attendant in charge of all cabin crew approached Dad and whispered in his ear. They were to stay on-board as all other passengers deplaned, they would then be taken to the VIP lounge where they would be met by the President's chauffeur and taken to the Official Residence. Their luggage would be collected and brought separately.

And so they arrived at the President's mansion, LOS PINOS, in grand style; exhausted but elated and excited. They were greeted by the First Lady and escorted to a reception room where they were provided cool drinks and delicious tasty 'nibbles'. George and Amy looked about in stunned amazement, they had visited Buckingham palace in London with their Nana and Grampa and seen the grand rooms of State but this room was bigger, higher and grander than anything they had seen in London.

The First Lady smiled, "Unfortunately, my husband is away for two days but has insisted you are to be accorded the full attention of the household staff, anything and everything you desire is yours for the asking. He has arranged a special visit for you tomorrow."

George and Amy jumped to their feet and in excited voices demanded, "Where are we going?"

Mum, Dad and the First Lady laughed, "Please," Amy squealed, "Where are we going?"

"A very special, very old and magical place called TEOTIHUACAN."

George and Amy tried to get their tongues around the strange word but without success. The First Lady gently took their hands and said, "Watch my lips and say it after me. TEO – TEWA – KAN."

After a couple of practices they had it and ran around repeating it time and time again until Mum said, "Okay you guys, that's enough."

"But what does it mean?" asked, George, "And what is it?"

"It's an ancient city, over two thousand years old." The First Lady replied, "But no one lives there now, but there's plenty to see. Pyramids, wide streets big enough for cars and trucks, tall buildings…"

"But why build wide streets? They didn't have cars then and my Grampa told me horses didn't arrive in South America until the sixteenth century when the Spanish Conquistadors arrived."

The First Lady was delighted, "Well done, George, correct on both accounts. So why did they build big wide roads? That's one of the mysteries of Teotihuacan. And there's something else." The children leaned forward in expectation… "There are secret tunnels and passages."

George and Amy were so excited that Mum and Dad thought they would never sleep but after a run around in the garden and a super dinner they discovered the President shared their Dad's interest in PINBALL games and so after a few exciting games they climbed the stairs and found their bedroom.

It was a massive room containing two FOUR-POSTER beds, a table and chairs for breakfast and their own private bathroom. The First Lady explained that she thought George and Amy would feel more comfortable in this strange house if they shared the room but if not there were other rooms available, about twenty in fact. Everyone shouted "NO." And so it was that George and Amy settled down to sleep in beds almost as big as their bedrooms at home.

They were awoken by the maid saying, "Buenos días, niños" as she opened the curtains and bright sunshine flooded the room. Breakfast of Orange juice, cereal, milk, fresh fruit and a cup of warm tea was laid on the table.

They washed, cleaned their teeth and got dressed one thousand times faster than they had ever, ever, managed on a school morning back home and were downstairs waiting for the car in next to no time at all.

It was only about forty miles to Teotihuacan, less than an hour in the luxury limousine, but the First Lady had kindly arranged for a few games to be provided and the screens in the seatbacks were bigger than the biggest iPad, so the time went very quickly and soon they were presented with a magnificent view of the PYRAMIDS at Teotihuacan.

As they climbed from the car, Dad said, "What first?" Amy and George looked at each other, and together said, "Last to the top is a stinky poo." And they ran off towards the pyramid and started to run up the stone steps. "How many steps, George?" cried Amy. A panting George, bent over, hands on knees looked at his sister, "Two hundred and forty-eight!"

"Are you sure, George?"

"Well I'm not doing it again, Amy, so if you want to check you can do it." Just then Mum and dad arrived. "Did you count the steps?" asked, Amy. Too exhausted to reply, Mum and Dad just shook their heads.

At two hundred feet high, the pyramid provided great views for miles around. At the very, very top was what looked like a chess board set into the stone, sixty-four squares, some dark, almost black, others white just like limestone. If it was a chess board the chess pieces would have to be as big as George and Amy because if they stood on a square it took a big long stride to move to another. They pretended to play chess for a few moments until suddenly, without warning, the board opened-up and they found themselves tumbling down a chute in complete darkness. Amy cried out in alarm, George shot out a hand and managed to grab her arm. "Hold on, Amy."

* * *

CHAPTER THREE.

They landed on a pile of straw, stunned, they looked about. The black darkness had been replaced by a brightness that almost hurt their eyes. But they could not see where the light came from.

They got to their feet and holding hands walked towards a tunnel entrance that was the only way in or out of this room which contained nothing but the large pile of straw upon which they had just landed.

The tunnel seemed to slope downwards and as they entered and moved forward they felt it getting warmer; ahead was a bright light and they could hear a noise, a sort of hum mixed with a whirr, George and Amy looked at each other and Amy huddled a little closer to her big brother. Something made them stop and turn around. Amy squealed and gripped George's hand even tighter; the tunnel behind them was completely black, black as a coalmine, not a light in sight. "George, where has the light gone?" Amy asked.

"I don't know, Amy, it's, it's just gone."

They turned back, fearful that the tunnel ahead might also have turned dark but they were relieved to see it as bright as ever. They decided there and then to not take any chances and began running along the tunnel just in case the light went out. They rounded a bend and came to a complete stop. It was a dead-end. Nowhere to go. Just a smooth wall blocking their way. They turned around, this time they both yelped in surprise. Nothing. Just black blackness. The light that accompanied them along the tunnel had gone. They spun around, the wall in front of them and the ceiling were still shiny and bright but the light did not spread to behind them.

"I don't understand this, Amy, how can light just stop? And where is it coming from? The wall looks so smooth it could be glass."

"Maybe it is Glass, George." Amy said, "And maybe it lets the light through from the other side."

They inched forward until they were inches from the wall; George put his hand out to feel it and nearly stumbled as his hand went straight through. He pulled it back quickly as if it was red hot.

"Did it hurt?" Amy asked. George shook his head. Then he aimed a quick kick, his foot went through. He looked at his sister. "Come on, Amy." He grabbed her hand and together they marched through the wall and into A HUGE DOME SHAPED ROOM.

"WOW!" they both said together as they looked about them. George turned to look at the wall they had just walked through, he reached out to touch it and felt a solid surface. He rapped it with his knuckles. "I guess we can't go back the way we came."

They had another look about. In the centre of the room was a round table. In front of the table stood two chairs. There was nothing else anywhere. Amy moved closer to George and put an arm around him, "Where are we? George, what is this place? I don't like it."

And then they heard it, a voice, loud but friendly,

"Welcome and do not fear, you are in no danger." They spun and looked around but could see no one or from where the voice had come. Then George pointed, "Look, Amy." Two squares of light had appeared on the floor. "Please stand on the squares." The voice commanded.

"Why" Demanded, George.

"It is necessary if we are to proceed. Please, there is nothing to fear."

"Who are you?" said George, "Where are you?"

"All will be explained in a few moments, but first you must move to the squares."

They looked at each other and shrugged before moving to the squares. "Thank you" the voice said.

George's square remained lit, Amy's went dark. Moments later a bright light from above completely encased George and seemed to swirl around him like white vapour. It lasted about 30 seconds and then went off. Before they could say or do anything the same process happened to Amy; when her light went off the voice said, "Hello George and Amy, welcome to Ptolemy. Please make you way to the two chairs and make yourselves comfortable. George, please sit on the left and Amy, you on the right."

As they settled in the chairs a lot of things happened. The table, until now completely flat and unadorned, became home to several flat screen monitors that popped up from within, as well as dials and sliding buttons, flashing lights and meters and things they hadn't seen before. The walls in front of them became huge screens but most interesting and exciting of all was the dome above them; it became a massive map of stars.

"It's a planetarium." Exclaimed, George. "May I ask a question?"

"Of course."

"What is this place and why is it called after a famous mathematician and Astrologer?"

"That's two questions, George, but never mind. What is this place? It's what you might call a control centre but it's also a beacon for travellers. Why is it called Ptolemy? Well it seemed a good name seeing as this control centre helps people navigate the stars and planets. This is but one of several million beacons that are situated throughout this and other galaxies."

"How do you know our names?" asked, Amy.

"I know everything about you, that's why I needed you to stand on the squares so the scanners could do their work."

"You still haven't told us your name, where we are or what you want from us." George said in a strong voice.

"As to where you are; you're still in Mexico inside what is now known as the 'Pyramid of the Sun'. Regarding my name, well it is in fact, AI-456-6900-T54 though I imagine you were thinking along the line of what you refer to as a noun, something like Amy, or George in which case you can call me ART, many others have.. And finally, what do we want from you? Nothing other than a little of your time and the use of your body and brain."

The children looked at one another in alarm. "Our body and brain." Whispered, George. Imagining they were about to be used for some horrible experiment.

"What are they going to do to us, George?" Amy cried in fright.

"Where are you, Art? Come out and show yourself" George demanded in his most authoritative voice.

"I cannot do that George because I do not exist, at least not in the way you mean, I am not a person I am a machine..." Before Art could finish, George jumped down from the chair in excitement,

"Your name, Art, short for Artificial Intelligence, the AI at the beginning of that long name you gave us before."

"You are quite correct, George."

"So this is just one big machine and no one else is here?"

"That is correct, George."

"How long has this machine been here?"

"That is not an easy question to answer in a way that makes sense for you."

"Try." said, George.

"One year for you, is the time it takes earth to travel once around the sun. Our galaxy is many light years away and our orbit takes ten thousand of your years to travel just once around your sun." George looks up at the dome's roof as he calculates...

"Wow! That means one day for us is about 30 years for you."

"Correct, George, I was built many thousands of your years ago, long before your planet became inhabitable and we therefore had to wait several millenniums until we could build beacons here on Earth."

"But the ancient Mexicans, Incas and Aztecs built the pyramids..."

"Yes they did, George, but with a little help from us."

"Us?"

"We are an ancient race that constantly travel the universe, visiting every galaxy, we have no home and remain nowhere for more than a few days, local time, a matter of hours in our time. But we must maintain the beacons in good order to help the millions of other travellers of every race that move around the galaxy.

Amy who had been listening suddenly breaks her silence, "I'm hungry... and thirsty."

A panel on the desk in front of Amy lit-up and there was a 'ding', a little like the sound of a lift before the doors open. The panel opened and a tray loaded with fruit and bread and a large glass of strawberry milkshake slowly came up through the opening. Amy's eyes opened wide with astonishment, "Wow! How did you know that's just what I wanted?" She asked.

"We know everything" Art replied. "How about you, George, are you hungry?" George laughed, "You said you know everything... You tell me."

A panel in front of George opened and a tray of food appeared. "One salad baguette and a cup of Tea. OK?" George gasped in surprise. "I guess you really do know everything."

They scoffed down their food as Art showed pictures on the screens of the pyramid being built. Through a mouthful of food, George said, but cameras hadn't been invented two thousand years ago..."

Art laughed, "Well spotted, George, quite true, but don't forget we are much older and we have ways of recording pictures and events that you don't even know about and will not for many thousands of years."

George and Amy sat back in their chairs and wiped their lips, the food and drinks were good and their hunger and thirst satisfied they wondered what was to happen next. Almost as if Art could read their thoughts the lights in the dome suddenly dimmed and the astral display above them seemed very much brighter. One star, or was it just a blip of light, was much brighter than all the others and it was moving across the domed ceiling, not fast, not slow but at a speed that was quite noticeable. "What's that?" they said together.

"That is HELIOS. A spaceship named after Hyperion's son, he was the Greek God of the Sun. That's not it's real name of course because it set off from its home many thousands of years before the Greeks wrote and told stories of the Gods, but it has to be called something you can pronounce and in a language you understand because the planet it comes from does not have a spoken or written language, communication is by thoughts alone."

Helios could be seen moving steadily across the dome. "Where's it going?" asked George.

"It's coming here." Art answered.

"Can we see it?" cried, Amy.

"That's why you are here." Art said, "You have an important role to play in the journey Helios is making across the Universe."

"When can we see it?" shouted Amy. By now the dot of light that is Helios is right overhead, almost the exact centre of the dome.

"You won't actually see it." Art said. The children groaned in response. But Art continued, "It's many thousands of miles away, a light year in fact. But you will go aboard."

"How can we do that?" George said, "If it's so far away"

Art made a noise that could have been mistaken as a gentle laugh. "I'm sure you have watched many space films and seen how people move from ship to ship or travel to the planet's surface."

"Transporters!" George and Amy said together.

"Exactly,." Art said. "Let's go, there's no time like the present."

A hidden door in the wall opened with a gentle hiss and the children walked through to what could only be called the TRANSPORTER ROOM. It was just as they had seen in films and on television. They stood on a round platform surrounded by glass walls and waited for what seemed a very long time even though it was only about twenty seconds. Amy grabbed George's hand, "George, I'm frightened."

"Don't worry, Amy, everything is fine. There's nothing to worry about. I promise."

The lights went out, the room became black. Amy squeezed George's hand, the lights came back on and they were surprised to see a very different room. A girl's voice said, "Welcome to Helios. Please come through."

A door in the wall opened and they stepped off the transporter platform and walked through to another room filled with monitors, screens, instrument dials and lots of equipment they could only guess at what it was used for.

A huge window looked out at the vast emptiness of space, in the distance small blue dot.

The girl's voice said, "That is planet earth. It is one light year away."

"How many miles is that, George?" Amy asked.

"About six trillion."

A noise behind made them turns. A beautiful woman entered the room. She had long blonde hair, green eyes and was dressed in a long red robe with gold braiding and a high collar that encircled her neck and touched her ears. She smiled, "Thank you for helping us, you are very kind."

"You're welcome." Said George, "Just tell us what you want us to do."

"We have a little time before we need to do anything, let me show you around. Would you like anything to eat or drink?"

"May I have an apple, please? Amy answered.

The woman smiled, "By all means, Amy, Red or green?"

"Red. Please." The woman indicated a small panel in the wall, it opened and there was a beautiful apple. "My name is, Hyperion, this ship is named after my son."

George hesitated a moment before asking, "Are you very old? You don't look old but..." The woman laughed and held out her hand, "Feel my skin."

George stroked her hand and was surprised when he felt nothing; in fact his hand just went straight through hers. He tried again, this time on her arm, then her shoulders, he tried to give her a hug. Nothing. He jumped back in alarm.

"Don't be frightened, George. Our race has evolved to the point where we are pure energy and do not require a physical body. Think of me as what you call a HOLOGRAM."

They spent a while being shown around the ship, every room was more exciting than the previous room. They were shown recordings of the formation of planets and stars millions of years in the past and of many strange looking creatures from different worlds. They even got to talk over a video link with the ruler of a planet that was like earth but so far away they would never be able to travel between each other for hundreds of thousands of years.

After they had explored the ship and watched films and even played a game of FOUR-DIMENSIONAL chess, Hyperion told them it was time to do what they had come to do. They returned to the control room, or flight-deck as a film would call it. "What do you want us to do, Hyperion?" George asked.

She pointed to what looked like a clock but it had twenty-one numbers, not twelve and only one hand that swept round, not two.

"It's important you watch that very closely." She pointed to a red chair, "George, sit there please and Amy, you sit in the blue chair. I want you to watch the hand sweeping round, when it crosses the number seven, George, you must hit that green button in front of you on the desk; and Amy, when the hand gets to fourteen you are to hit the pink button in front of you; AND most important of all, when it reaches twenty-one you are BOTH to hit the TWO buttons in front of you, George the GREEN and YELLOW and Amy, the PINK and PURPLE. They must all be pressed at the same time. UNDERSTOOD?"

The children nodded, Hyperion smiled, "Ready, set... GO!" The clock hand swept down past one, two, three, four... when it got to seven George hit the green button, the clock hand carried on to eight, nine, ten it got to fourteen and Amy hit the pink button, the hand carried on to twenty-one and the children hit all four buttons together in perfect timing,

They jumped back in surprise as lights flashed everywhere and a recorded voice announced, "All systems re-set. Guidance on-course. New data uploaded. Journey recommences in three minutes."

Hyperion clapped her hands, "Well done, children, we needed your small and real hands to do that, without your help this journey could not continue. Now it is time for you to return to the Dome but before you go we have gifts for you." A panel in the wall opened to reveal two objects. A wrist-watch for George and a pendant-watch for Amy.

These are special gifts for special children, they will never need batteries and will always tell the correct time, but if you pull the button out and turn it three times it will show you where in the universe HELIOS has travelled and exactly where we are. Now quick we must transport you back to the dome before you become trapped on board.

They said goodbye to Hyperion in the transporter room and moments later they were back in the dome and watching the dot that is HELIOS travel across the roof of the dome.

* * *

CHAPTER FOUR.

"Well done Children." Art told them, "Your help today will be talked about until the 'End of Time' your courage and deeds will be recorded and generations of countless races will forever be in your debt, ships, universities, cities even will be named in your honour; a million years from now you will be talked about with reverence."

"But we only pressed a few buttons." George interjected,

"And because you did so, Helios was able to continue its journey through countless galaxies, delivering hope, knowledge, advice and new life to generations old and new and will continue to do so for millions of years."

"LOOK!" Shouted, Amy, and pointed at Helios as it raced across the Dome's roof, "It's leaving our universe." The dot of light that was Helios disappeared off the roof; suddenly they felt alone and the room went quiet.

"Before you go, there is one more task I would ask of you." Art said, "But this time the task is not without a little danger and thus it is your choice as to whether you can fulfil my request."

"What do you mean by danger?" George asked, "I'm responsible for my sister, I mustn't put her in harm's way..."

"I understand that, George." Replied Art, "But by danger I mean nothing more than perhaps a bump on the head and a couple of scratches."

"What do we have to do?" Amy asked a little nervously.

A whirring sound attracted their attention and out of a panel in the wall, they watched a box about the size of a cereal packet slowly emerge until it stopped about three feet from the wall. They heard a small sound, almost like marbles rolling around.

"When you asked me what this place is, I told you "A Beacon", as I am sure you will understand, beacons send and receive signals but to do so requires power and unfortunately the power-source in this beacon has developed a fault and must be replaced. This is where you two come in."

"So where's the danger?" George asked.

The sound of a door opening made them turn and look behind them, a door had opened in the wall and through it they could see a long staircase, "That door leads to a tunnel and stairway to the very top of this pyramid."

"But we're at the top, we climbed all 248 steps, I counted every one of them." George exclaimed.

"Yes you did, but when the chessboard opened and you slid down the chute you travelled much further than you imagined."

"How far?" Amy asked in a small voice.

"About six hundred feet." Art told them.

"But that means we're four hundred feet underground." George said, "Cool!"

"How are we going to get out?" Amy wanted to know.

"This is where the danger comes in." Art replied, "And it's your final task."

"What do we have to do?" They said together.

They listened carefully as Art explained everything and gave them instructions about what to do and when and, most important of all, what NOT to do, because that's when the task would become dangerous.

They picked up the box and as they prepared to leave the dome they were stopped by Art saying, "I also have a little gift for you both." They turned and moved towards the desk where yet another hidden door had popped open. They looked inside and removed what looked like two small torches. They turned them over and over in their hands but could not see any button or lamp bulb. "What are they?" George asked.

"They don't really have a name that would mean anything to you but let's call them Kwikcoms. When you see a bright moving light in the night sky, just point the device at the light and say something, anything, 'Hello' would be a good start, and if that bright light is a traveller, you will get a reply and be able to talk together, whichever planet or galaxy they are from and wherever they are .

"Wow!" they both said together. "One more thing" Art said, "and this must be kept secret, "if you hold it when someone from another country talks to you in their own language, you will be able to understand them as well as talk back in their language. But they will only work with you, if someone else holds them nothing will happen." They said goodbye to Art and set off for their final and, just possibly, dangerous task.

George went first, through the door and up the long staircase. Amy was close behind. It wasn't a spiral staircase but a square cut one, meaning there was ten steps to a small landing where you turned left then climbed another ten steps to anther landing and another left turn and another ten steps and so on and so on.

Exhausted and out of breath they reached the top; they sat on the last step to recover. "One thousand and ninety, before you ask." Panted George.

"I counted one thousand and eighty nine." Replied Amy.

"The correct number is one thousand and eighty eight." Came another voice.

George and Amy looked at one another, no longer surprised at mysterious voices from nowhere.

"Who are you?" They said together.

"I am the Guardian" the voice replied.

"The Guardian of what?" Amy asked

"The Eternal Guide."

George and Amy looked at each other in surprised confusion, "But Art sent us up here to fix the Power Source. What's the Eternal Guide?" George asked.

"They are one and the same. Open the box and you shall see."

Amy opened the box and they both peered in. There was about a hundred glass balls, each the size of a large pea and six about the size of a tennis ball. "Art has explained what you have to do." George and Amy nodded.

"Then it is time." A sound of cogs and gears grinding together made them start and they watched in amazement as the walls around them folded flat exposing the outside world. Amy squealed in fright. They were suspended in mid-air. Absolutely nothing beneath their feet but fresh air and fifty feet down was the top of the pyramid.

"Art did not explain the invisibility?"

"No!" they said together.

"Never mind, in the box are special glasses, put those on now and all will be revealed." They took the glasses from the box and slipped them on and to their surprise could see the spire on top of the pyramid that they had climbed. Now they understood the instructions that Art had given and began fixing the glass balls around the spire. They both wore harnesses that they had taken from the box; Amy had to hand them one by one to George as he climbed up and down the spire. Sometimes Amy had to climb up to him other times he had to slide down to her. It was hard and difficult and if it wasn't for the harnesses, very dangerous. After about an hour they had finished fixing the glass balls, all one hundred and six.

Because they could only hear and not see the Guardian they did not know where to look so in a loud voice, George enquired, "What now, Guardian?"

"Your work is finished. Well done, George and Amy, it's time for you to move on."

"Move on?" They said together.

"Press the button on the side of your glasses."

When they did so, something else happened; a zip-wire appeared between the top of the spire where they had just fixed the glass balls and a building way down on the other side of the street and far away from the pyramid. "Just hook your harnesses onto the runners and off you go."

"Is it safe?" Amy asked

"Perfectly" Said the Guardian, "and until you detach from the wire, you will remain invisible, just as you are now."

It was the ride of their lives, zooming down the wire at great speed, the wind blowing through their hair with a whooshing sound and everything around them just a blur. As they approached the end of the wire, a door opened in the building and they slid inside, landing on a soft pile of feathers. The door closed behind them. For a few seconds it was dark and then a light came on and they saw they were in an empty room.

"Hello, George and Amy." They didn't bother to look around; by now they were used to disembodied voices coming from nowhere and everywhere, they just sat and waited for the next instruction.

"Hello you two, over here, behind you."

They turned and saw an old woman, possibly the oldest person they had ever seen. She was about five foot tall, one and a half metres if you prefer, with long grey hair that reached past her waist. Her skin was very wrinkled and the colour of old parchment, if she had a hook nose they would have thought her a witch but she didn't, it was small and pert and she had the most vivid blue eyes you have ever seen and the whitest teeth in the world. She looked very kind. She smiled.

"Well. Are you going to sit there all day? Come over here and toss the glasses and harnesses in that box."

* * *

CHAPTER FIVE.

They walked towards the old woman. She smiled, "Hello, I'm Teotlalco."

They struggled to get their tongues around the name, she laughed,

"It's not so difficult; try this, THEO-LAL-COH."

They laughed and after a couple of attempts they had it. "But who are you?" Amy was quick to ask.

"I'm here to help and guide you home."

"But we live in England." said Amy. The old woman nodded,

"I know that, Amy, what I mean is back to your parents and the house of the President. But first we thought you would like to see how my people lived five hundred years ago and how we came to work with Art and The Guardian."

"You know about them?" George said, but they're not people they're machines."

"Yes they are." Said Teotlalco "But once, many thousand years ago, they were people, or at least they were built by people to carry on their work until the end of time."

Amy screwed up her nose and pulled a face, "The end of time? Art said the same thing. What does it mean? If it's the end of time it's the end of everything and everyone." George looked open mouthed at his sister, "Wow, Amy, that is awesome. Real cool. I couldn't have said it better myself."

Teotlalco smiled and clapped her hands, "Well said indeed, Amy, it's just an expression, a little silly if you ask me, it's just another way of saying "A very long time.""

"So how are you going to show us your people?" George asked, "They lived five hundred year ago and there's no such thing as a time machine."

Teotlalco smiled and said "That's true but there is another way, a way that is better and without danger. Do you know about 'Virtual Reality'?"

"Yes!" they shouted, "We've got one at home, Dad bought it."

Teotlalco nodded, "I'm not surprised, but what I have is better. Come with me and I'll show you." She led them through a door and down a long flight of stairs, through another door and into what could only be called a huge cave. In the centre of the cave was a large glass ball with two seats inside it. She led George and Amy to the ball and settled them comfortably on the seats. "I'll come and get you later." Moments after she left it seemed to grow dark until there was nothing to see except each other.

Amy reached out and clasped George's hand and then, without warning, the glass surrounding them disappeared and they found themselves sitting in the centre of a town square. All about them people went about their daily lives; market traders, butchers and fishmongers, grocers with piles of fresh vegetables and others selling cheese and milk. A carpenter was fixing the roof on a nearby cottage and a stonemason was high on a scaffold putting the final touches to a great tower. No one took any notice of George and Amy though they looked very much out of place in their trendy twenty-first century clothes whereas everyone else wore very little, just enough in fact to keep them warm when the sun went down. They all had shoes made of wood and leather and without exception all had an abundance of jewellery, mostly gold and sparkling stones about their bodies. Some even had colourful headdresses and one in particular had one that marked him out as someone special, a leader or chief, maybe even an Emperor or King.

Excited and intrigued by all they saw about them, George and Amy approached a market stall that displayed huge apples, "¿Cuánto son las manzanas?" Amy asked in her best Spanish but got absolutely no response. She went to pick up the apple but her hand went straight through it and the market stall. "They're holograms" George cried, "They can't see or hear us and we can't touch them or anything we see because they don't exist."

Hand in hand they moved around the town going in and out of the various houses and buildings; one must have been the

Town-Hall or something like that because there was a long table with at least twenty serious looking and very old men sitting in high back chairs all speaking in loud voices and to one side an even older man was attempting to write down what was being said. It was great fun watching and knowing they could not be seen or heard.

In a house a young woman was cooking over an open fire and in another a man was baking bread. As they returned to the town square they noticed Teotlalco sitting on the wall that surrounded the town fountain, "Hello George, Hello Amy, What do you think of my home?"

"How can you see us?" Amy asked, "George said everything was just a hologram."

"Except me." She laughed, "Now I want to show you something special, come with me."

She led them through a door and down some stairs, "Everywhere we go means going up or down stairs." George grumbled, hearing this Teotlalco turned and whispered, "These are the last ones, I promise." After what seemed a very long time and hundreds of stone steps they came to a dark tunnel, Teotlalco reached up and removed from its place in a special holder, a large 'torch' and from a small hole in the wall a flint.

She struck the flint and with the sparks lit the torch. They headed off down the tunnel, the flames from the torch casting long strange shadows behind them. Suddenly

Teotlalco stopped and George and Amy bumped into her. "It's a dead-end." They said together.

"Is it?" said Teotlalco, "look closely."

Amy went left and George right and they looked very closely. "Yep, it's a dead-end." Amy declared. "I agree." said George, "Definitely a dead-end."

Teotlalco pulled George and Amy to the right hand side, pointed to a spot about a foot above Amy's head and whispered, "Push here," as they did, the wall seemed to move. They pushed harder and the whole wall swivelled and they found themselves on the other side of the tunnel wall.

They were in another cave, Teotlalco moved around lighting the many torches fixed to the walls, about twenty all together, the cave was flooded with light and they gasped in surprise. All about them was an abundance of treasures. Precious metals, jewels, sculptures, goblets, plates, scrolls of ancient parchment and books,

"The treasures and history of my people, the Aztecs" Teotlalco told them as a tear gently rolled down her cheek "One day, perhaps, they will rise again and restore their power and wisdom to this continent but until then this must remain hidden." She went to a small casket and removed two medallions on gold chains that she then hung about Amy and George's neck. "Take these as a small token of your visit and assistance today. Now I'm sure you both must be very hungry and perhaps even a little tired." They both nodded and followed her through to another cave where they saw a great feast laid out on a big table and near the other wall a huge bed.

After a sumptuous meal they jumped on the bed and before anytime at all were both fast asleep.

* * *

CHAPTER SIX.

Sunlight flooded into their room as the maid opened the curtains, "Buenos días, niños".

George and Amy jumped up and looked around the room in confusion they remembered going to sleep in the treasure cave but now here they were back in their bedroom at the Presidential mansion.

Breakfast was on the table. Orange juice, cereal, milk, fresh fruit and a cup of warm tea. Amy whispered to George, "Did you dream about Art?" he looked at her is surprise and nodded "And the Guardian."

"What about the zip wire?" she said

"And the treasure cave." they said together. But we can't have had the same dream." George said, "It's impossible." They looked at one another for a few moments and then together said, "The presents."

They ran across to their clothes that were neatly folded on a chest next to their bed and rummaged through them. "Look." said Amy and pulled out the 'pendant watch' she was given by Hyperion aboard Helios, and then the medallion from Teotlalco.

"It wasn't a dream" George shouted, holding up his watch, "It was real, it really happened. But how did we end up back here? And what about Mum and Dad, they were with us at the top of the pyramid steps, but then we fell down the chute in the chessboard, if they didn't see us fall why didn't they tell us off for disappearing?"

"Or ask us where we'd been." Chipped in Amy.

Just then, Mum and Dad entered their room, "Come on you two." Said their Mum, "Your first day here we thought you would be up and ready by now and impatient to get off to TEOTIHUACAN."

"But we went yesterday," Amy started to say until George elbowed her in the ribs. "We'll be down in five minutes, Mum." George said.

As they left, Dad said, "Don't be long we've got a full day ahead, lots to see and do."

As he closed the door, George and Amy looked at each other and then at their presents, "It did happen, Amy, it really did. Otherwise how else could we have got these?"

They quickly got dressed, ran down stairs and met up with Mum and Dad in the courtyard and jumped in the car that was taking them to TEOTIHUACAN.

Mum and Dad were puzzled that George and Amy did not appear excited at seeing the pyramid for the first time and were not shouting and asking questions.

They ran up the stone steps (again) but when they reached the top they were surprised to find the 'chessboard' was nowhere to be seen..

"Where's the chessboard?" they asked the guide who looked at them in astonishment.

"How do you know about the chessboard? No one has ever seen it - in fact most experts believe it is just a legend, a mythical chessboard that transports players to another world."

Just then someone shouted "LOOK!" and everyone looked up to the sky as a bright light zoomed across leaving a small white trail. It was much too high to be an aircraft and too bright to be a shooting star.

As everyone was watching the mysterious light, George took Amy behind a rock and together they pulled their Kwikcoms and pointed up towards the bright light.

"Hello" they said together, and then looked at their watches given them by Hyperion, instead of seeing a 'star map' of Helios's journey through the Galaxy they were treated to the face of a very old man who looked like he was out of one of those wizard story books.

"Hello, Amy and George, my name is Methuselah, not the one the Bible, though he was named after me. I lived many thousands of years before those Biblical times and it was I that designed and built ART and HELIOS and those devices Hyperion gave you. Perhaps you would understand better if I explained that in my world, one single day is like one million of your years so, as I believe you have already learned in other stories, nothing is as it may at first appear and thus understanding 'Time' is far more difficult than most people know.

For example, I know of another world where one of their days is equal to ten million of my years. But that's not why I speak with you today. Normally we would arrange things so that you would wake up and have no memory of your adventures - but we were so pleased with your efforts and willingness to help we decided your reward is to keep your memories and gifts but only if you promise to never tell anyone of what you have done. Nor must you ever show anyone what those devices are capable of."

"What are you two doing hiding behind this rock?" Their Dad's voice made them jump.

"Nothing, Dad", they quickly jumped to their feet and tried to hide their watches,

"What do you have there, you little monkeys? Let me see." But when George showed Dad his wrist and Amy her pendant, there was nothing to be seen, at least by Dad, that was, they could still see their watches but to everyone else they were invisible.

"Come on, we have to be moving on, there's lots more to see."

They spent the entire day exploring and amazed their guide, as well as Mum and Dad, by their seemingly expert knowledge of the ancient peoples that lived and built the pyramids and surrounding buildings and roads.

Of course they couldn't say how they knew so much but they really enjoyed answering all the questions the guide asked. At one point, in one of the old cottages they saw an old woman sitting in the shade, she smiled at them and put her finger on her lips, as if to say 'Shush, don't say anything', for a moment they thought it was Teotlalco, they looked at each other in excited surprise but when they turned back, she was gone.

They arrived back at the Presidential mansion exhausted and after telling the President's wife all about their day over a sumptuous meal they charged upstairs for a bath and bed. Just as they were closing their eyes, their watches 'buzzed'. They pulled out the knobs and watched as Helios moved across the face.

They looked up at the sky and saw a tiny glow and unlike anyone else on earth knew what it was, not a star, not a comet and not an asteroid. It was a spaceship travelling through the galaxy, providing help and assistance and knowledge to countless planets, repairing damaged beacons, building new ones and ensuring that every planet in every universe in every galaxy was kept safe and out of harm.

They went to sleep knowing that without their help none of that would have been possible. As Hyperion said, "Their name would forever be remembered."

Maybe, in time, the 'Milky Way' will be renamed, 'THE GEORGE & AMY STARBELT.'

THE END.

(Or maybe it's just the beginning.)

CPSIA information can be obtained
at www.ICGtesting.com
Printed in the USA
BVHW031410120422
634079BV00003B/137